YECK ECK yeck eck

YECK ECK

written and illustrated
by Evaline Ness

E. P. Dutton & Co., Inc.
New York

LIBRARY OF CONGRESS CATALOGING IN PUBLICATION DATA

Ness, Evaline.   Yeck eck.

SUMMARY: A young girl loves babies so much
that she saves up to buy one.

I. Title.

PZ7.N4384Ye   [E]   74-3406   ISBN 0-525-43470-4

Published simultaneously in Canada by Clarke,
Irwin & Company Limited, Toronto and Vancouver
Printed in the U.S.A.   First Edition

10 9 8 7 6 5 4 3 2 1

To Ann Durell + Albert & Margot

This small person, Tana Jones, had everything she wanted except the thing she wanted most.

A REAL BABY.

Tana loved all babies: black, white, yellow, brown, fat, skinny, awake or asleep. Whenever she met one she stopped to talk to it. Unfortunately, they were always attached to mothers.

So Tana asked her father, who drove a taxicab all over the big city, to pick up an unattached baby for her. Mr. Jones refused. When Tana asked why not, he said, "You can't go around just picking up babies like Pepsi caps, that's why not. So get it out of your head."

But that is exactly what Tana couldn't do: get it out of her head.

One night before going to sleep Tana's head whispered, "Why don't you save your money and *buy* a baby?"

The next day she started right in to take her own advice. She stopped buying candy, ice cream, and bubble gum. Every penny she saved went plunk into a coffee can until one day she counted up to $5.00. "Wow!" said Tana. "That should buy a pretty good baby."

So out she went shopping.

But she had no luck.

One, two, three, four, five, ten mothers all said the same thing when Tana offered to buy their babies: NOT FOR SALE!

Then Tana remembered her friend Arnie Wizbee. Arnie had so many little brothers and sisters, he no doubt would be *glad* to sell one. So Tana hopped over to Arnie's house.

To her surprise, Arnie wasn't selling. He was *giving!* He told her to pick out one and welcome to it. He said, "Call it a gift."

While Tana was making up her mind, a baby crawled over and sat on her foot. He looked up at her and yelled: YECK ECK! Tana understood perfectly. It meant: TAKE ME!

Joyously, Tana carried Agift home. They ate cookies and drank milk. Tana gave Agift a bath and washed his clothes. Then she put him to bed in her doll carriage.

When Mr. Jones came home from work, Tana flung herself into his arms and cried, "I just got a baby! It's Agift!"

Mr. Jones pulled his cap down over his eyes and staggered about the room. "Help!" he moaned.

The second time that Tana got a baby to keep was when she was pushing Agift in the carriage. A lady came up to her and said, "Please take care of Albert. I must go away."

Tana was delighted. She let Albert push the carriage all the way home. When they got there she put them both in the bathtub and let them wash each other.

Mr. Jones, coming home and finding another baby, heaved a sigh. "A gift, I suppose?"

"Of course not!" said Tana. "This is *Albert!*"

Then two odd things happened. In one week the doorbell rang twice. Each time Tana opened the door there was nobody except a baby with a note pinned on it. Each note said: PLEASE TAKE CARE OF MY BABY. Both babies had said: YECK ECK. So Tana did.

She named them Sunshine and Moonbeam.

Now Tana had four babies. She fed them and bathed them. She sang them to sleep and washed their clothes. Her clothesline grew longer and longer and her days grew shorter and shorter.

Every afternoon Tana took her babies to the playground. She slid them on the slides. She swung them in the swings. She tried to teach them to talk. But they just laughed and said: YECK ECK.

Tana's father, however, did *not* laugh. He said: YICHHHH! He had to work overtime, including Saturdays and Sundays, to make more money for tons of cookies and oceans of milk.

One shiny afternoon at the playground, Tana met Mr. Doowell. He walked over to her and took off his hat. He bowed low. Then he invited her and her babies to meet *his* babies. He said he had fifteen and expected more.

When they arrived at Mr. Doowell's house there were, indeed, fifteen babies. Tana kissed each one and introduced them to Agift, Albert, Sunshine, and Moonbeam.

Then she sang songs, stood on her head, and taught them their faces.

They knocked at doors, peeped in, lifted latches, walked in, and went way down cellar and ate apples until they got so tired they fell asleep in a heap. Agift, Albert, Sunshine, and Moonbeam were asleep too. They looked so comfortable Tana decided not to disturb them.

"I'll pick up my babies tomorrow," Tana told Mr. Doowell.

Early next morning Tana gobbled her breakfast and sped to Mr. Doowell's house. She played hide-and-go-seek-I-gotcha all day long with the babies.

gotcha

When it was time to leave, Agift, Albert, Sunshine, and Moonbeam screamed. They screamed all the way home. When Tana tried to comfort them, they screamed harder and louder.

At last Tana screamed back, "WHAT DO YOU WANT!"

"We want to go back to Mr. Doowell's house," said Mr. Jones.

Tana stared at her father. She stared at the screaming babies. "I don't believe it!" said Tana in a choked voice.

But she *did* believe what she heard when they reached Mr. Doowell's house: SILENCE.

Mr. Doowell bowed to them all. He turned to Tana and said he was honored and privileged to care for her outstanding babies. He also said he would be most grateful if she could promise to visit often.

Tana wanted to cry more than she wanted to promise. But promise, she did.

Then she kissed Agift, Albert, Sunshine, and Moonbeam good-bye. They all laughed and yelled: YECK ECK!

Tana stood back and eyed them. She frowned. "What *does* YECK ECK mean?" she asked herself.

Herself answered, "Don't ask *me!* Only a *baby* knows!"

EVALINE NESS is a distinguished author-illustrator of many picture books. She received the 1967 Caldecott Medal for *Sam, Bangs & Moonshine*; her Dutton titles are: *The Girl and the Goatherd, Do You Have the Time, Lydia?* and *Don't You Remember?* (written by Lucille Clifton). Miss Ness studied at the Art Institute in Chicago and the Corcoran School of Art in Washington, D.C.

Miss Ness recalls that as a little girl in Pontiac, Michigan, she loved babies so much that she would actually borrow them from the neighbors and, like Tana, bathe them, give them cookies, and put them to sleep in her doll carriage. But they always had to be returned after a few hours—hence this story of the way she *wished* it had been.

The display type is a combination of hand-lettering, Stymie Extra Bold, and Helvetica. The text type was set in Century Schoolbook. The three-color preseparated art was printed by offset at Pearl Pressman Liberty.